S0-BSJ-285

BABAR'S
MYSTERY

Laurent de Brunhoff

Babar's Mystery

Harry N. Abrams, Inc., Publishers

People come from all over the world to Celesteville-on-the-Sea for its beautiful beaches. King Babar and Queen Celeste were vacationing at the Grand Hotel with their children—Pom, Flora, and Alexander. They strolled the

promenade that runs along the shore.

"Wait for us," Arthur and the Old Lady shouted from the terrace. The Old Lady planned to write a novel while on this trip.

The sun was strong, so big umbrellas lined the beach. Some bathers played, some relaxed, and others splashed in the water. Babar and Celeste were happy. The Old Lady, however, thought it was too crowded and noisy.

"I need quiet and solitude to write my book," she said.

"You can work in the lighthouse," Celeste told her. "You will hear nothing but the splash of waves and the cries of gulls."

The Old Lady, delighted by the suggestion, left at once with her cat, her typewriter, and a stack of paper. Babar and Celeste went along with her on their bicycles. Arthur arrived

When they returned to the hotel, Babar, Celeste, and Arthur heard the children shouting.

"The piano has been stolen! Some furniture movers took it away." Flora showed everybody a glove she had found on the sidewalk.

"If we can just find the owner of the other glove, we will have the thief!"

"A valuable clue," cried Arthur. "I will start an investigation at once."

The Old Lady had decided to remain at the lighthouse until evening. So Babar and Celeste went to the market to buy her lunch—some fruit, bread, tomatoes, and ham—while Arthur questioned the glove merchant.

"Madame, have you recently sold a pair of gloves like this? It belongs to a thief, we think."

"No. But I think that my friend Patamousse at Mont Saint Georges sells some like it. Go see him."

The Old Lady had asked that absolutely no one bother her while she wrote her novel. So Babar sent the lunch up for her in a basket, using a rope and pulley.

Arthur arrived and reported on his investigation.

"We will all go to Mont Saint Georges," Babar decided.

Babar drove the whole family—except Arthur—in his shiny red car. Mont Saint Georges, imposing behind its thick stone walls, is only a few miles away from Celesteville-on-the-Sea.

"You know," said Alexander, "at high tide Mont Saint Georges is surrounded by water—just like an island. You have to take a boat to get there."

Babar parked the car and walked toward the castle ramparts with Celeste, Pom, Flora, and Alexander. Arthur made sure that his motorbike was safe.

What a crowd! Tourists came to Mont Saint Georges in busloads.

The narrow streets were full of sightseers looking at all the souvenir and antique shops. Babar, Celeste, and the children pushed through the crowds until Arthur located the shop of Patamousse the glove merchant.

"Sir, have you sold a pair of gloves like this one?" he asked the hippopotamus.

Unfortunately, the merchant had sold many such gloves. "But," he said, "I seem to recall that the last customer to buy a pair like that was a lion."

"Ah," said Arthur, "perhaps he is my thief."

Pom, Flora, and Alexander had grown tired of walking, so the whole family sat down at an outdoor café to eat some delicious crêpes, a specialty of the region. Arthur seemed thoughtful. He had noticed a rhinoceros at a neighboring table.

"That is a suspicious-looking fellow," he whispered. "Do you think he might be one of the thieves?"

Celeste told him not to suspect people just because of the way they look.

"You must have other, better clues," said Babar. "Being a detective is difficult."

At last it was time to leave, and the family walked away from the castle ramparts only to find that their car had disappeared!

"Where is my car?" cried Babar. "Someone has stolen my car!"

He went around asking all the bus drivers if they had seen his red car. One of them remembered seeing a red car driven by a crocodile. Another remembered a lion. A third remembered an elephant at the wheel.

"Which one should I believe?" Babar wondered.

"Come, we will have to go back to Celesteville-on-the-Sea by bus."

Back at the hotel Babar gathered his family around and told them, "In a little while a new gold statue is going to be unveiled at the Celesteville Seashore Theater, and I must give a speech. A big crowd will be there. I want you to keep your eyes open."

Right away Pom, Flora, and Alexander went off to the theater.

Outside it, the decorators were hanging beautiful garlands of flowers in the town square. One of them, a lion, walked past with a box under his arm. On his left hand he wore a glove—just like the one Flora found!

Was he the thief?

Pom, Flora, and Alexander rushed off to tell Arthur the news.

"The lion decorating the square must be the one who lost the glove! So he must also be the one who stole the piano! And the car, too!"

Quickly they returned to the square with Arthur, who stood in the doorway of the theater to observe from a distance. But now the lion, high on a ladder, had put on his other glove. So he was not the thief.

Later on, Babar delivered his speech in front of the statue, which was covered with a sheet. Arthur watched the crowd of spectators, hoping that some new clue would put him on the trail of the thieves.

Finally Babar said, “And I wish much joy to all the future audiences at the Celesteville Seashore Theater.” Then, raising his trunk, he prepared to uncover the statue. Everyone held his or her breath. At last they would see the gold statue!

Babar gave a sharp tug at the sheet, the cloth slid off . . . but NO STATUE! Someone had stolen it! In its place stood a crude dummy made from a barrel and some pieces of wood.

"Catch the thieves!" shouted the crowd.

"First the piano, then Babar's car, and now the statue!"

Arthur jumped on his motorbike and drove it onto the main road. As he turned the corner, he spied a red car speeding away . . . Babar's car! On the backseat there was a large, peculiar-looking bundle.

"That must be the statue," said Arthur. "I've found the thieves! I won't let them get away this time."

Where did they go? Arthur lost the trail at a street corner.

Since he was on the road to the lighthouse, he stopped to see the Old Lady.

He wanted to ask her if she had heard a car go past.

"You are looking for a thief in Babar's car?" exclaimed the Old Lady.

“I did hear a car just now. It must have stopped very near here.”

What was going on in that little shed? They heard laughter, then a piano.

Arthur snuck up quietly and put a large box under the window.

He climbed up onto the box and peeked into the shed. . . . What did he see?

Four crocodiles danced with joy around the statue, which shone with a golden light. Babar's car was there, and the piano, too! One of the thieves, the one wearing a glove, cried out with a sneer, "Ha! Ha! Ha! I would have liked to have seen Babar's face when he discovered the barrel and the pieces of wood!"

"Hurry up," said another. "We must not be late to our meeting at the harbor."

Arthur had learned enough, so he slipped away. He wanted to get to the harbor ahead of the crocodiles.

From his hiding place, Arthur saw the crocodiles climb aboard a boat with a rhinoceros whom he recognized as the one eating ice cream at Mont Saint Georges!

"Good work, my friends," the rhinoceros said. "Here in this briefcase is half of the money I promised you. You will get the rest when you deliver the loot at my place on the other side of the bay. You can keep the piano for your hideout."

Arthur rowed away quietly in his little boat to warn Babar. He would know what to do.

That night, the crocodiles loaded most of the loot onto a boat. They thought they had been very clever. They did not suspect that Arthur and Babar were watching them from a hiding place behind the lighthouse.

Suddenly, at a signal from Babar, the Old Lady, who was on watch at the top of the lighthouse, began to shout, "Stop, thieves!"

The crocodiles stopped in their tracks, flabbergasted.

"There is somebody up there," one of them shouted. "But it is only the Old Lady!"

"Ah-ha! Old Lady!" yelled the crocodiles. "No one can hear you. Ha! Ha! We will take you away with us on the boat. You won't have a chance to tell Babar about our business." The four crocodiles rushed into the lighthouse after the Old Lady.

That was exactly what Babar was waiting for. The minute they were in the lighthouse, he slammed the door. The Old Lady climbed into the empty basket, and Arthur lowered her to the ground. Now the crocodiles were prisoners! Arthur rushed off to get some help, while the four thieves cursed their bad luck.

The next day everyone on the beach read the newspaper account of the exciting event:

ROBBERS CAPTURED!

Discovered by Arthur and the Old Lady, the robbers—a gang of four crocodiles—have been arrested, thanks to King Babar's bold strategy. The courage of our dear Old Lady has won everyone's admiration. The leader of the gang, a rhinoceros, intended to sell the statue and leave in Babar's car. The Coast Guard caught him while he was trying to escape. The theft of the piano was the idea of the crocodiles, who are, in their spare time, musicians.

Library of Congress Cataloging-in-Publication Data

Brunhoff, Laurent de, 1925-
Babar's mystery / by Laurent de Brunhoff.
p. cm.
Summary: While vacationing at Celesteville-on-the-Sea, the Babar family matches wits with a bold gang of thieves.

ISBN 0-8109-5033-2
[1. Elephants—Fiction.] I. Title.

PZ7.B82843Bac 2004
[E]—dc22

2003024533

Published in 2004 by Harry N. Abrams, Incorporated, New York.

Printed and bound in China

10 9 8 7 6 5 4 3 2 1

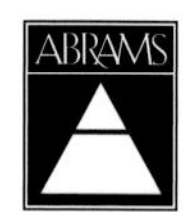

Harry N. Abrams, Inc.
100 Fifth Avenue
New York, NY 10011
www.abramsbooks.com

Abrams is a subsidiary of

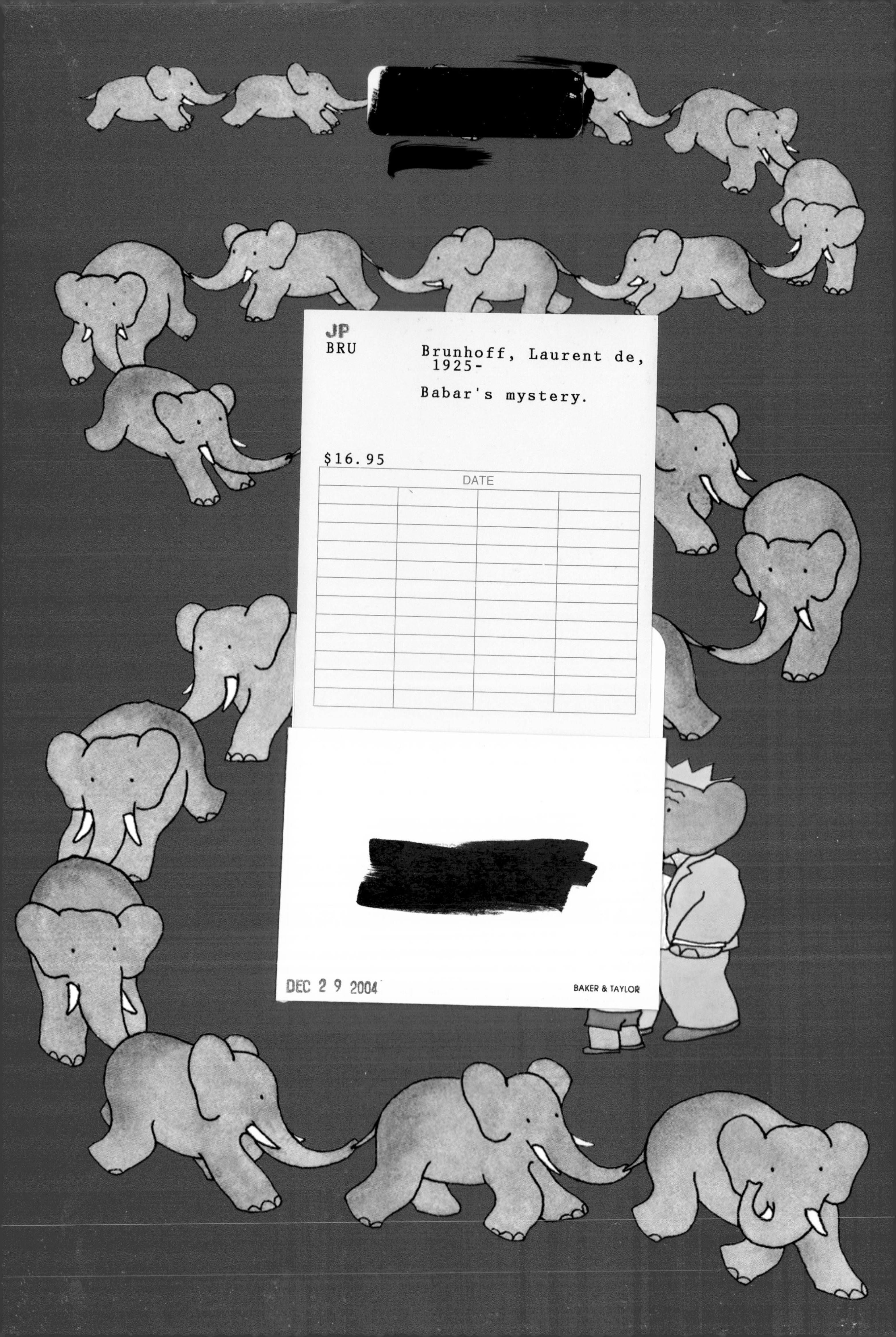